HANS CHRISTIAN ANDERSEN
THE SNOW QUEEN

A new adapted version by Naomi Lewis

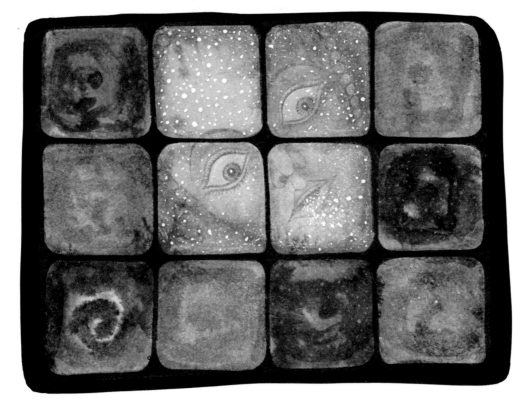

ILLUSTRATED BY
ERROL LE CAIN

THE VIKING PRESS   NEW YORK

To John Cook ... in gratitude

ELC

First American Edition

Text adaptation Copyright © 1968, 1979 by Naomi Lewis
Illustrations Copyright © 1979 by Errol Le Cain

Published in 1979 by The Viking Press
625 Madison Avenue, New York, N.Y. 10022

Printed in Great Britain

1 2 3 4 5 83 82 81 80 79

Library of Congress Cataloging in Publication Data

Lewis, Naomi.
   The Snow Queen.

Adaptation of *Sneedronningen*.

   Summary: The strength of a little girl's love enables her to overcome many obstacles and
free a boy from the Snow Queen's spell.

   [1. Fairy tales] I. Andersen, Hans Christian, 1805–1875. *Sneedronningen*. II. Le Cain, Errol.
III. Title.

PZ8.L4812Sn 1979   [E]   78–10462
ISBN 0–670–65378–0

NCE, in a great town, lived two poor children.

THEY were not brother and sister, but they were just as fond of each other as if they were. He was called Kay, and she Gerda. They lived next door to each other, in attics at the tops of two houses; they could step across and meet in the strip of roof between. Each attic home had a small side window, one facing the other. Outside each window a rosebush had been planted in a wooden pot. The trailing branches met overhead, and under them the children sat and played.

One summer the little girl learned a song with a verse about roses, and she sang this to the little boy:

> "In the vale the rose grows wild;
> Children play, all the day.
> One of them is the Christ-child."

In winter, when white snowflakes covered the roof, the grandmother told them of the Snow Queen, who flew through the dark clouds and covered the windows in icy patterns.

"If she came here," said Kay, "I'd put her on the stove and she would melt!" But grandmother smoothed his hair and told them other tales.

One day, Kay told Gerda, "Grandmother says I may take my sledge to the big square with the other boys."

The game the boys liked best was to tie a sledge to the back of a farmer's cart, and so be carried along.

On this day, while the boys were playing, a great white sleigh came into the square, driven by someone in a thick fur cloak and white fur hat. Kay quickly tied his little sledge to the big sleigh, and started to ride behind. They went faster and faster, out of the square and into another street.

Whenever Kay began to untie the rope, the driver would turn round and nod in a friendly way, so Kay was still there when the sleigh drove out of the city gates. Kay was afraid, and managed to loosen the rope at last. It was no good – the little sledge still sped after the big one; they flew like the wind. Kay called out for help, but no one heard. Suddenly the falling snowflakes parted like a curtain.

THE great sleigh stopped and the driver rose. It was a lady, tall, slender, brilliantly white – the Snow Queen herself!

"We have travelled far and fast," she said. "But you are cold!"

She lifted Kay beside her, and put her white fur cloak around him. He felt as if he were sinking into a snow-drift. Then she kissed his forehead. Ah! The kiss was colder than ice. It went straight to his heart.

But then the strange feeling passed. He seemed to feel perfectly well, and he no longer noticed the cold. Once again the Snow Queen kissed him – and he forgot little Gerda and all his life at home.

KAY looked at the Snow Queen; he could not imagine a wiser or lovelier face. And she flew with him high up into the dark storm clouds, while the wind whistled and roared as if it were singing old ballads.

Over forest and lake they flew, over land and sea. Beneath them the cold blast shrieked, the wolves howled, the black crows soared over wastes of glittering snow.

But high over all shone the great clear silver moon, and Kay gazed at it all through the long winter night. During the day he slept at the Snow Queen's feet.

BUT what did little Gerda think when Kay did not
return? What had become of him? she wondered. No one
knew. Gerda wept bitterly. It was a long, sad winter. But
spring came at last and the warm sunshine.

"I shall put on my new red shoes," she said early one
morning, "and I'll go down to the river to ask about
him."

She kissed her sleeping grandmother, and went out,
quite alone.

"Have you seen my playmate Kay?" she asked the
waves. "I'll give you my new red shoes if you give him
back to me."

The waves seemed to nod in a strange fashion, so she
climbed into a boat that lay in the reeds, took off her
shoes and threw them as far out as she could. But the
waves carried them straight back to her.

Then she became aware that the boat was floating away from the shore, for it had not been moored fast and went gliding away, gathering speed all the time.

"Perhaps the river will carry me to little Kay," Gerda thought, and she sat still, watching the pretty banks. There were flowers and trees and fields of sheep and cows, but not a single person anywhere.

AT last she came to an orchard of cherry trees; in the middle was a little house with blue and red windows and a thatched roof, while standing outside were two wooden soldiers who presented arms whenever anyone passed.

Gerda called out, and from the house appeared an old, old woman, leaning on a crooked stick. She was wearing a large sun hat painted all over with wonderful flowers. She caught the boat with her hooked stick and drew it to the land.

"You poor child!" she said. "However did you come to be floating here all alone in the great wide world?"

WHEN Gerda had told her story, and asked if she had seen little Kay, the old woman said that he had not passed there yet, but would surely come by later. Then she gave the little girl some cherries and combed her shining hair with a golden comb . . .

The memory of Kay began to fade from Gerda's mind. For the old woman was a witch, though not a wicked witch. She used magic only now and then for her own amusement, and just now she very much wanted to keep little Gerda with her.

Then she went into the garden and touched all the rosebushes with her stick, and they sank deep down into the earth without a trace.

SHE feared that if Gerda saw roses she would think of her own on the roof, and so remember little Kay and go on with her journey.

AFTER that she took the little girl into the garden. How lovely it was! There were flowers of every kind, of every season in the year. Gerda jumped for joy, and played among them till the sun went down behind the cherry trees. She played there the next day, and the next.

But as time went on, it seemed to her that one kind of flower was missing. Which could it be? She was looking at the old woman's sun hat with the painted flowers when she saw that the loveliest flower on it was a rose. The old woman had forgotten about this.

GERDA ran to the garden and searched and searched for roses, but in vain. Her tears began to fall just where a rosebush lay buried, and the bush sprang up again full of beautiful blossoms.

GERDA now remembered little Kay.

"Oh, I have lingered here too long," she said. "Roses, do you know where Kay can be? Is he dead and lost to me for ever?"

"No," said the roses. "We have been under the earth, and he was not there. Kay is not dead."

"Oh, thank you, thank you," said Gerda, and she ran out of the garden and into the wide world.

SUMMER had gone; it was autumn, cold and sad. The yellow leaves fell, one after another, in the damp, misty air.

"I have lost too much time," thought Gerda. "I dare not stop."

But at last, tired out, she sat down to rest. And there, hopping towards her, was a large friendly crow. She asked him if he had seen little Kay.

"Caw!" said the crow. "Could be! Could be!" And he told her about a boy who had come out of nowhere with creaking boots and a bundle on his back and had won the hand of the princess of that kingdom.

THE crow promised to take Gerda into the palace after
dark by a little back staircase, so that she could see the
boy for herself.

At nightfall the crow returned, and Gerda followed
him through a great garden, where the leaves were
falling, falling, to the back of the palace, where a door
stood slightly open. As she climbed up the staircase
something seemed to be rushing past along the wall –
shadows of lords and ladies, many on horseback. These
were the dreams of the sleeping people.

At last she came to a wonderful room where two beds,
each made to look like a lily, hung from a thick stem of
gold. In one lay the princess, in the other a boy – but it
was not little Kay.

"You poor little thing," said the prince and princess
when they heard her story. They gave her clothes of silk
and velvet, as well as warm boots and a muff for the
journey, and set her in a carriage of pure gold, packed
with fruit and sugar sticks and gingerbread nuts.

Then they wished her good luck, and waved as the
coach sped away.

The forest they drove through was dark as night, but
the coach shone like the sun, and it dazzled the eyes of
the robbers lurking there.

"It's gold! It's gold!" they shouted, and they dashed
forth, stopped the horses, and dragged out the little girl.

A HORRIBLE old robber woman tried to seize her, but her daughter, a dark-eyed little robber girl, jumped on the old woman's back and made her stop.

"She shall play with me," said the little robber girl. "She shall give me her muff and pretty clothes, and sleep with me in my bed. And I shall ride with her in the coach."

The robber girl was so spoilt and wilful that she always had her way. She climbed into the coach with Gerda, and they drove off deep into the forest. She put her arm round Gerda and said, "They shan't kill you as long as I don't get cross with you. You are a princess, I suppose?"

"No," said Gerda, and told of her search for little Kay. The robber girl looked thoughtful; she dried Gerda's eyes, and put her own hands into the soft warm muff.

THE coach stopped at the courtyard of a ruined castle. Ravens and crows flew out of holes in the walls. Inside, a large fire was burning in the middle of the stone floor. The smoke rose to the roof, and had to find its own way out. A great cauldron of soup stood over the fire and was bubbling away.

When they had finished a good supper, the robber girl took Gerda to a corner where blankets and straw were scattered.

In the rafters above, hundreds of doves were roosting.

"These are all my pets," said the little robber girl. "And there's my own special sweetheart, Bae." She pulled a reindeer forward by the antlers. He had a bright copper ring round his neck, and was tied to the wall by a rope.

"We have to keep him fastened," said the robber girl, "or he would be off in a flash, back to the snowy North Land he loves."

She took a long knife from a crack in the stone, and then pulled Gerda into bed with her. "I always sleep with my knife by me," she said. "You never know what may happen. But now tell me once again about little Kay, and your journey into the wide world."

So Gerda told it from the beginning, and the doves listened too. Then the robber girl put her arm round Gerda's neck and slept. But Gerda was much too afraid to close her eyes.

Then the doves said, "Rr-coo! Rr-coo! We have seen little Kay! He was sitting in the Snow Queen's sleigh when it flew over the forest where we lay in our nest. She must have been going to Lapland, for there is always ice and snow there. Ask the reindeer; he knows."

"Ah, yes," said the reindeer, and his eyes grew bright, "that is a lovely country, full of snow and ice. You can run about freely in the glittering frosty valleys. I was born there: who should know better than I? That is where the Snow Queen has her summer palace. Her real home is near the North Pole."

Gerda sighed. "Oh, Kay, poor Kay," she murmured. But she dared not disturb the robber girl.

IN the morning Gerda told what she had heard, and the little robber girl looked very serious.

Then she said to the reindeer, "I should like to keep you here, but I'm going to set you free so that you can take the little girl to the Snow Queen's palace, where she can find her friend. You've heard what she has been telling me." The reindeer leapt for joy.

The robber girl lifted Gerda onto his back, and even gave her a little cushion to sit on.

"Here are your fur boots," she said, "but I shall keep your muff – it's so pretty. Still, you won't be frozen – I'm giving you my mother's big gloves; they'll reach up to your elbows. And there are two loaves of bread and a ham for you, so you won't starve. Now, off you go," she said to the reindeer, "but take good care of the little girl."

Gerda held out her hands in the big gloves and called good-bye, and the reindeer leapt over bush and briar, over marsh and moor, as fast as ever he could. The wolves howled, the ravens screamed, and the Northern Lights flashed through the sky.

FASTER and faster the reindeer ran, day and night alike. The ham and loaves came to an end – and then they were in Lapland.

THEY stopped at a little hovel, whose door was so low that people had to crawl on the ground to get in or out. There they found an old Lapland woman who stood frying fish over an oil lamp, and the reindeer told her Gerda's story.

"You poor things!" said the Lapland woman. "You've a long way to go yet – hundreds of miles. But first you must call on the Finland woman; she can tell you more than I can. I'll write her a word or two on a dried cod, for I haven't any paper."

So off they went again, on, on, until they reached the Finland woman's house.

It was so small that they knocked on the chimney. But – my! how hot it was inside. The woman helped Gerda to take off her gloves and boots; then she laid a piece of ice on the reindeer's head; last, she read what was written on the codfish. Three times over she read it, then put it in the cooking pot, for she never wasted anything.

But she spoke never a word.

"You are so clever," pleaded the reindeer. "I know you can bind all the winds of the world in a single cord. Won't you give the little girl a magic drink so that she can overcome the might of the Snow Queen?"

The woman drew him into a corner, and whispered: "I can give her no greater power than she has already. Don't you see how, everywhere, men and beasts have to serve her? And how wonderfully she has made her way in the world alone on her two small feet? Little Kay is bewitched by the Snow Queen. He remembers nothing of Gerda and his home. Only Gerda's love can win him back. Now, a few miles from here the Snow Queen's garden begins, and you can carry the little girl as far as that. Put her down by the big bush with red berries – you'll see it in the snow – then hurry back here!"

The woman lifted Gerda onto the reindeer's back and off they sped.

"Oh," cried Gerda in the biting cold, "I've forgotten my boots and my gloves!" But the reindeer dared not stop; he ran till he came to the bush with the red berries, and there he set her down. He kissed her, and tears ran down the poor animal's cheeks, but he had to turn back again.

There stood Gerda, with bare feet and hands in the terrible Northern cold.

She hastened on, then saw that an army of snowflakes seemed to be moving towards her. They ran along the ground in strange white ugly shapes, growing larger all the time; they were the Snow Queen's frightful sentinels.

Little Gerda began to say the Lord's Prayer.

Her breath made a mist in the freezing space, and shaped itself into a host of small bright angels holding spears. They struck at the dreadful snow creatures which fell into thousands of pieces. They touched Gerda's hands and feet, and she no longer felt the cold.

On she went towards the Snow Queen's palace.

But where was little Kay all this time?

He was in the great cold palace. The walls were of driven snow; the doors were of cutting wind. The snow had formed into more than a hundred enormous halls; all were vast, empty, glittering, and icy cold. The largest was many miles long; in the midst of it was a frozen lake, and there the Snow Queen liked to sit when she was at home.

Little Kay was blue with cold – yet he did not feel it, for the Snow Queen's kisses had turned his heart into a lump of ice. He was alone in one of the great empty halls, playing with pieces of ice and making them into patterns.

The Snow Queen had said to him, "If you can make the pieces of ice spell the word Eternity I shall set you free and give you the whole world, as well as a new pair of skates." Then she flew off to lay some snow on the high peaks of Etna and Vesuvius.

But, try as he would, Kay could not make the word. And that was how Gerda came upon him at last as she wandered through the palace.

She flung her arms round his neck and cried out, "Kay! I have found you after all!"

But Kay sat there quite still, stiff and cold. Then Gerda wept hot tears, and they pierced right through to his heart and melted the ice. She began to sing:

"In the vale the rose grows wild;
Children play, all the day.
One of them is the Christ-child."

And Kay cried out, "Little Gerda, dear little Gerda, where have you been all this time? And where have I been, too? How cold it is here, how huge, how empty!" He hugged her, and they laughed and cried for joy.

Even the pieces of ice shared their happiness. They danced about, and when they lay down again they formed the word that the Snow Queen had told him to make: Eternity . . . He was free!

Kay and Gerda took one another by the hand and made their way out through the halls of the great palace. Wherever they went the winds lay still and the sun broke through the grey clouds. They reached the bush with the red berries – and there was the reindeer waiting for them with a sleigh.

He carried Kay and Gerda to the home of the Finland woman, where they warmed themselves, and learned how to find their way home.

Then they went on to the Lapland woman, who came with them to the boundaries of the cold country. There they parted from the woman and the reindeer, with many a fond farewell.

AND, as Gerda and Kay stepped forward, they saw the
first green shoots of spring. The birds began to twitter,
and out of the forest rode a girl on a splendid horse, with
a pair of pistols, and a red cap on her head. It was the
robber girl on her travels into the wide world; the horse
was from the golden coach.

"You're a fine one," she said to little Kay. "I wonder
if you deserve to have someone running to the end of the
world for your sake!"

But Gerda smiled, and asked her to call on the prince
and princess when she passed that way, and find out how
the crow was faring, too.

THEN Kay and Gerda walked on, hand in hand. All around them the woods were beautiful with flowers and fresh green leaves.

At last they saw in the distance the high towers of their own city, and heard the church bells ringing.

On they went till they came to their own street, and the stairs to Grandmother's door. Everything stood in the same friendly place. The clock ticked comfortably, the roses growing across the roof waved in at the open window, and Grandmother smiled with joy to see them. It was just as if they had never been away.

Kay and Gerda sat in the sunshine under the roses, and both thought of the old song and the part it had played in their story:

> "In the vale the rose grows wild;
> Children play, all the day.
> One of them is the Christ-child."

The cold empty splendour of the Snow Queen's palace had gone like a bad dream. They were together, never to part again, and it was summer, glorious summer!